MW00902352

Let's Go, Milo!

A Book Of Outdoor Adventure

Valeri McCarthy

———

Wake up! Wake up!

Rise and shine!

Let's go. Let's go. Let's see what we can find.

Let's seize the day and adventure is a good way.

Let's kayak.

Let's camp.

Let's swim.

Let the fun begin!

Let's take a hike.

Let's ride a bike.

Let's go surf!

Let's go sail.

Let's scuba dive.

You can look for a whale!

Let's rock climb.

Let's snowboard.

Let's play ball.

You can do it all!

Let's run.

Let's raft.

Let's row.

It's time to get out and go!

Let's zipline.

Let's paddleboard.

Let's hang glide.

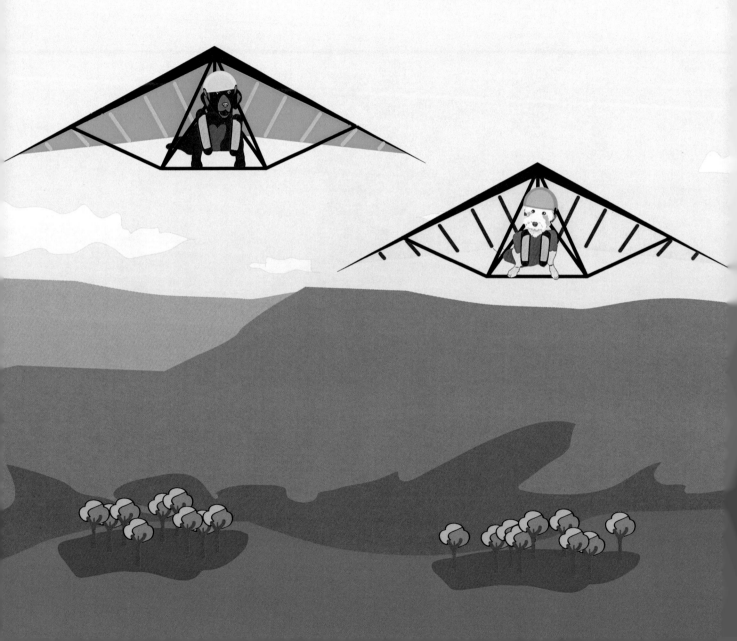

It's up to you to decide!

Let's go, Milo!
Let's see what we can do!

Let's go! Let's go!
How about *you*!

Let's Go, Milo!

A special thanks to Tim, Paige, Keeton & Mom.

Made in United States
North Haven, CT
18 April 2022